Ladybug Barber

Written by Sarah Toast

Illustrated by Elena Kucharik

Copyright © 2000 Publications International, Ltd.

ISBN 0-7853-1936-0

Leap Frog is a trademark of Publications International, Ltd.

Lucy Ladybug loves to cut hair. Every morning she makes her shop ready for the day.

Everyone in Bugtown wants to look terrific, so Lucy is very busy. Lucy washes one bug's hair while she cuts another's.

Soon Bessie Beetle comes to Lucy's shop with Becky, her daughter. Becky is excited about getting a haircut.

First Bessie and Becky get their hair washed and styled. Then they read magazines while they sit under the dryers.

Bessie loves her new hairstyle, but Becky's hair didn't turn out quite right. Lucy decides to try again.

Lucy comes up with the perfect style for Becky. It looks great!

"Lucy Ladybug, you're the best barber in Bugtown," says Becky as she waves good-bye.

Lucy can't wait for tomorrow, when more happy bugs will come to her shop for haircuts.